STAR WARS™

THE FORCE AWAKENS
GRAPHICS

EGMONT

We bring stories to life

First published by Hachette Livre in 2016
Published in Great Britain 2017
by Egmont UK Limited, The Yellow Building,
1 Nicholas Road, London W11 4AN

Translated by Edward Siddons

Direction: Catherine Saunier-Talec
Art Director: Antoine Béon
Project Manager: Anne Vallet
Design: Nicolas Beaujouan
Illustrations: Bunka
Production: Amélie Latsch

© & ™ 2017 Lucasfilm LTD.

ISBN 978 1 4052 8578 0
66930/1
Printed in Poland

For more great *Star Wars* books, visit www.egmont.co.uk/starwars

STAR WARS™

THE FORCE AWAKENS

GRAPHICS

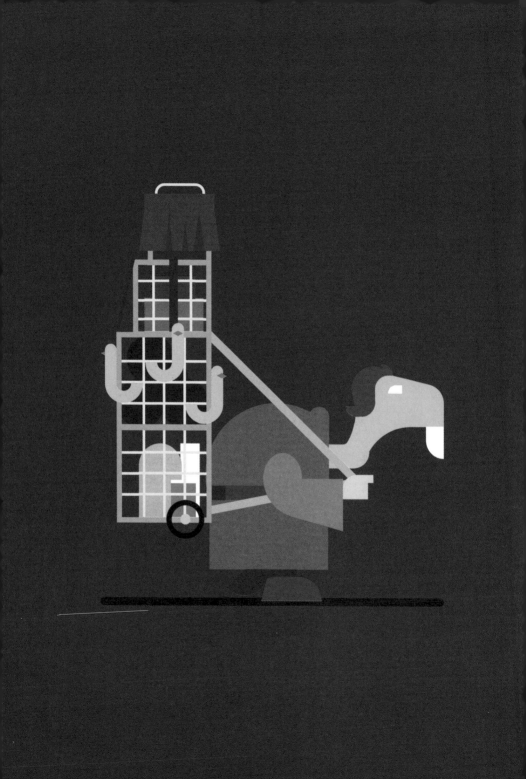

STAR WARS

INTRODUCTION

When *The Force Awakens* stormed into cinemas in December 2015, it had been 33 years since we first saw Luke Skywalker, Leia Organa and Han Solo defeat the Empire in *Return of the Jedi*. The latest instalment brought back some of our favourite characters, and introduced us to new heroes, loveable rogues and loyal droids.

While Episode VII opened up countless new possibilities, there are many links between *The Force Awakens* and the previous six *Star Wars* films. This book connects the past and present through engaging graphics.

Enjoy the infographics, and ready yourself for even more spectacular episodes to come.

CONTENTS

THE FORCE AWAKENS
IN NUMBERS

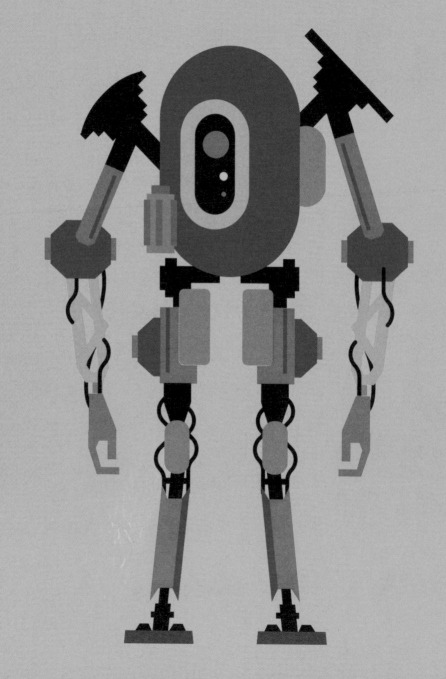

3 HEROES

1 LIGHTSABER

1 SPEEDER **2** BASES

1 SON

1 JEDI

3 LIGHTSABER BATTLES

2 GENERALS

1 LEADER OF THE FIRST ORDER

2 MERCENARY GANGS

1 DESERTER

1 MILLENNIUM FALCON

MAZ KANATA

1

3 RATHTARS

CHARACTER JOURNEYS

The heroes of the *Star Wars* Universe have always hopped from planet to planet. Here's a brief look at the characters in action in *The Force Awakens*.

TAKODANA

FIRST ORDER SHIP

ERAVANA

JAKKU

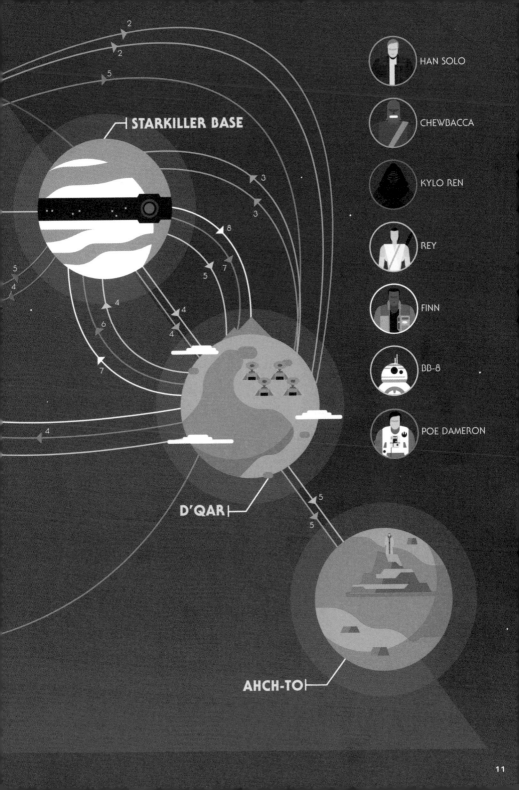

STARKILLER BASE

HAN SOLO

CHEWBACCA

KYLO REN

REY

FINN

BB-8

POE DAMERON

D'QAR

AHCH-TO

THE EVOLUTION OF
C-3PO

THE PHANTOM
MENACE

ATTACK OF
THE CLONES

ATTACK OF
THE CLONES

REVENGE OF
THE SITH

C-3PO is a legendary figure in the saga, largely due to his unique and instantly recognisable physical appearance. And yet, the famously rule-abiding droid has changed numerous times. The details of some of these transformations can be seen below.

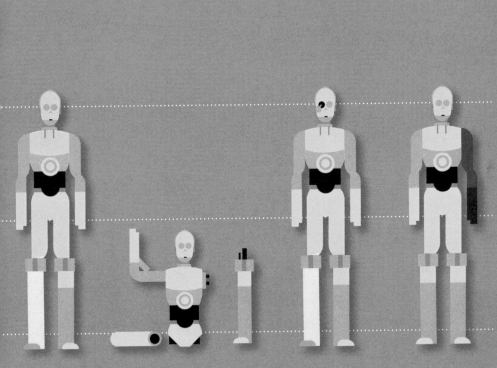

A NEW
HOPE

THE EMPIRE
STRIKES BACK

RETURN OF
THE JEDI

THE FORCE
AWAKENS

DROID
GENERATIONS

BB-8

TYPE	ASTROMECH
CATEGORY	BB SERIES
MANNED SPACECRAFT	X-WING T-70
EQUIPMENT	ATTACHMENT CABLES
	WELDING TORCH
	HOLOPROJECTOR
	ARC WELDER
	DATA COLLECTOR
	ALL TERRAIN
MASTERS	POE DAMERON

Like R2-D2, BB-8 is a trusty and charming droid who, with a few beeps and whistles, steals the show. Here is a look at how the two droids compare.

R2-D2

- ASTROMECH
- R2 SERIES
- DELTA-7B - ETA 2 INTERCEPTOR - X-WING T-65 - Y-WING
- -
- WELDING TORCH
- HOLOPROJECTOR
- ARC WELDER
- LIGHTSABER COMPARTMENT
- PERISCOPE
- DATA COLLECTOR
- ALL TERRAIN
- PADMÉ AMIDALA - ANAKIN SKYWALKER - BAIL ORGANA - OWEN LARS - LUKE SKYWALKER

FAMILY TREE
FROM SHMI TO KYLO REN

Beru Whitesun

.... Adoption

.... Love

——— Bloodline

Cliegg Lars

Owen Lars

Luke Skywalker

Shmi Skywalker

Anakin Skywalker

Breha Organa

Padmé Amidala

Leia Organa

Kylo Ren

Bail Organa

Han Solo

THE LIGHTSABER'S JOURNEY

THE STORY OF A ROUND TRIP

Obi-Wan retrieves the lightsaber from Anakin

Obi-Wan gives the lightsaber to Luke

Luke loses the lightsaber in Bespin

Maz gains possession of the lightsaber

Rey brings the lightsaber to Luke

Maz gives the lightsaber to Finn

Rey retrieves the lightsaber

PHYSICAL PROPORTIONS

FROM THE DEATH STAR TO STARKILLER

The Empire's army evolved into the First Order, which inherited its predecessor's ability to construct gigantic battle stations. How does the base built by Palpatine's army compare to that of the ghostly Snoke?

DEATH STAR

DEATH STAR II

STARKILLER BASE

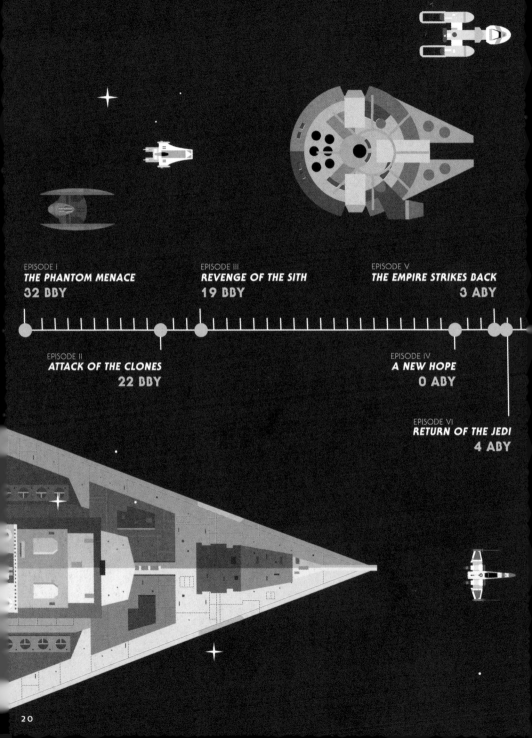

EPISODE I
THE PHANTOM MENACE
32 BBY

EPISODE III
REVENGE OF THE SITH
19 BBY

EPISODE V
THE EMPIRE STRIKES BACK
3 ABY

EPISODE II
ATTACK OF THE CLONES
22 BBY

EPISODE IV
A NEW HOPE
0 ABY

EPISODE VI
RETURN OF THE JEDI
4 ABY

THE *STAR WARS* TIMELINE

Our heroes have grown and changed, but how long has it been?
And how much time has passed since the Battle of Yavin in *A New Hope*?

BBY = Before the Battle of Yavin   ABY = After the Battle of Yavin

EPISODE VII
THE FORCE AWAKENS
34 ABY

KYLO REN

Kylo Ren fancies himself as the successor to his illustrious forebear, but does he possess the same qualities as Darth Vader?

HAN SOLO — **FATHER**

LEIA ORGANA — **MOTHER**

LUKE SKYWALKER — **MASTER (LIGHT SIDE OF THE FORCE)**

SNOKE — **MASTER (DARK SIDE OF THE FORCE)**

KNIGHTS OF REN — **AFFILIATION**

NUMBER OF DUELS SHOWN

Finn   Rey

ARTIFICIAL LIMBS

0

NUMBER OF LIGHTSABER BLADES

FILMS

ARTH VADER

ER   NONE

ER   SHMI SKYWALKER

IDE OF THE FORCE)   OBI-WAN KENOBI

IDE OF THE FORCE)   PALPATINE

IATION   SITH

F DUELS SHOWN

Luke

F LIGHTSABER BLADES

ARTIFICIAL LIMBS
4

CHARACTER QUOTES

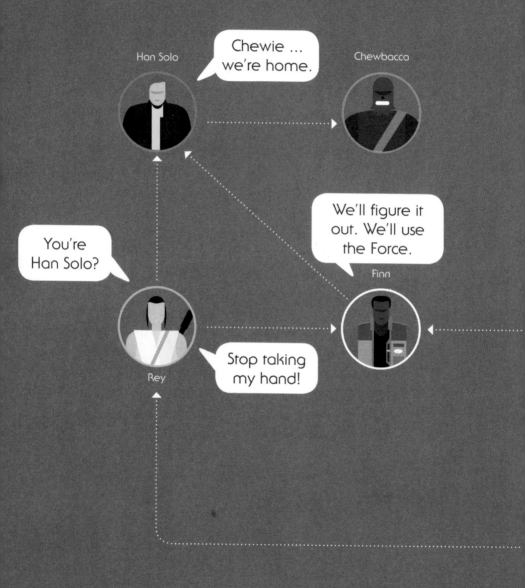

In the world of *Star Wars*, things quickly gain cult status, even what the characters say. In *The Force Awakens*, there are the usual references to missing droids and the recurring 'I have a bad feeling about this', but some new quotes have joined the fray. Here are a select few.

KYLO REN'S
RAGES

Kylo Ren is a sombre and mysterious character with an infamous lineage; however, he is incapable of controlling his anger. Here we return to the notable moments where Kylo Ren lost control.

"I'll show you the dark side!"

Kills Lor San Tekka on Jakku after he refuses to give up the map to Luke Skywalker.

"The droid ... stole a freighter?"

Destroys the control panel of the Resurgent-class Star Destroyer on hearing that BB-8 escaped with the map.

"Nooooooo!"

Destroys the interrogation room on the Starkiller Base after Rey's escape.

"That lightsaber. It belongs to me!"

Becomes furious when Finn ignites Luke's lightsaber and raises the blade.

CHARACTER
MEASUREMENTS

Happabore
2.30 M

Han Solo
1.80 M

Luke Skywalker
1.72 M

Poe Dameron
1.74 M

Rey
1.70 M

Maz Kanata
1.24 M

Chewbacca
2.28 M

Finn
1.78 M

C-3PO
1.71 M

Leia Organa
1.50 M

R2-D2
1.09 M

BB-8
67 CM

Snoke
?

Captain Phasma
2.00 M

Kylo Ren
1.89 M

General Hux
1.85 M

Unkar Plutt
1.80 M

CHARACTER
MEASUREMENTS

Grummgar
2.70 M

Stormtrooper
1.83 M

Bala-Tik
1.80 M

Tasu Leech
1.57 M

Bazine Netal
1.70 M

CHARACTER TIES

From the original trilogy to *The Force Awakens*,
history mirrors itself ... but not completely.

LUKE SKYWALKER --------→ REY

HAN SOLO ------→ POE DAMERON

R2-D2 ---------→ BB-8

OBI-WAN ------------→ HAN SOLO

MAZ KANATA -----→ YODA

DARTH VADER --------→ KYLO REN

THE EMPEROR --------→ SNOKE

GRAND
MOFF TARKIN --------→ GENERAL HUX

SARLACC ------→ RATHTAR

DEATH STAR -----→ STARKILLER BASE

FILMING
LOCATIONS

KRAFLA
ICELAND

STARKILLER

CUMBRIA
UNITED KINGDOM

TAKODONA

AHCH-TO —

D'QAR

SKELLIG MICHAEL
IRELAND

GREENHAM COMMON
UNITED KINGDOM

Did you recognise any of the shooting locations while watching *The Force Awakens*? Here is a handy map of the locations that form the backdrop of the new film.

JAKKU

ABU DABI
UNITED ARAB EMIRATES

NEW PLANETS

The Force Awakens introduced us to new worlds in the *Star Wars* Universe, from a remote desert planet to a mobile ice planet.

JAKKU
LOCATION: INNER RIM
LANDMARK: NIIMA OUTPOST

D'QAR
LOCATION: OUTER RIM
LANDMARK: RESISTANCE OUTPOST

TAKODANA
LOCATION: MID RIM
LANDMARK: MAZ KANATA'S CASTLE

HOSNIAN PRIME
LOCATION: CORE WORLD
LANDMARK: CAPITAL OF THE NEW REPUBLIC

AHCH-TO
LOCATION: ?
LANDMARK: ANCIENT RUINS

STARKILLER BASE
LOCATION: UNKNOWN REGIONS
LANDMARK: FIRST ORDER BASE

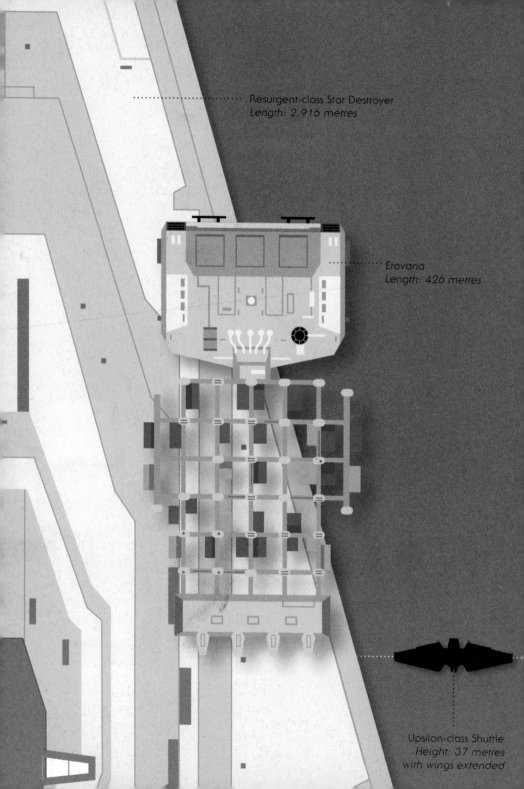

Resurgent-class Star Destroyer
Length: 2,916 metres

Eravana
Length: 426 metres

Upsilon-class Shuttle
Height: 37 metres
with wings extended

SPACECRAFT PROPORTIONS

Millennium Falcon
Length: 35 metres

X-wing T-70
Length: 12.5 metres

TIE fighter
Length: 6.7 metres

HUMANOIDS
AND OTHERS

This distant galaxy is teeming with numerous species. Based on the new characters introduced, here is a look at how the species are divided, calculated using the number of characters who have direct interaction with the heroes.

64.29%
HUMANOID

28.57%
ALIEN

7.14%
DROID

PHASE 1 CLONE TROOPER
REPUBLIC

1

EVOLUTION OF
STORMTROOPER
HELMETS

PHASE 2 CLONE TROOPER
REPUBLIC

2

3

STORMTROOPER
EMPIRE

PILOT   SCOUT TROOPER   SNOWTROOPER

FLAMETROOPER

PILOT   SNOWTROOPER

4

STORMTROOPER
FIRST ORDER

X-WING
VS X-WING

X-WING T-65

12.50 M LENGTH

●●●● ENGINES

☒ HYPERDRIVE

☒ DEFLECTOR SHIELDS

WEDGE ANTILLES

The X-wing fighters – and their stalwart pilots – were crucial to the Rebel Alliance in the Battle of Yavin and the Battle of Endor. In *The Force Awakens*, the Resistance's new X-wing fighter makes its debut.

X-WING T-70

LENGTH 12.48 M

ENGINES ●●●●

HYPERDRIVE ☒

DEFLECTOR SHIELDS ☒

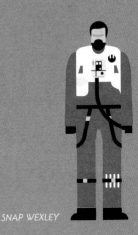

SNAP WEXLEY

TIE FIGHTER
VS
TIE FIGHTER

Has the exceptional combat craft significantly evolved since the fall of the Empire?

TIE/LN STARFIGHTER
AFFILIATION: GALACTIC EMPIRE

8.99 M LENGTH

●● ENGINES

NO HYPERDRIVE

REFLECTOR SHIELDS

SOLAR COLLECTORS

●● CANNONS
SFS L-S1

TIE/SF STARFIGHTER
AFFILIATION: FIRST ORDER

LENGTH 6.69 M

ENGINES ●●

NO HYPERDRIVE

REFLECTOR SHIELDS

SOLAR COLLECTORS

CANNONS ●●
S-JFS S9.6

THE FINAL BATTLE

What finally led to the downfall of the terrifying First Order army?

1 - Han Solo, Chewbacca and Finn block the Starkiller Base's shields.
2 - Rey escapes from prison and comes across Han Solo, Chewbacca and Finn.
3 - Kylo Ren kills Han Solo. Chewbacca detonates the mines he laid.
4 - Poe Dameron and BB-8 attack the Starkiller Base.

5 - Finn and Rey fight Kylo Ren.
6 - Chewbacca rescues Finn and Rey just before
    the explosion of the Starkiller Base.

UNKAR PLUTT'S
FINANCES

Surviving in the arid deserts of Jakku isn't easy; selling bits and pieces found among the wreckages littering the planet is the best way to make a living. Unkar Plutt takes these scraps in exchange for ration packs. Let's take a closer look at the prices demanded by the horrid Crolute.

Vegetarian meat substitute

Polystarch

SURVIVAL RATIONS
Stocks from the Republic
and the Empire

ONE QUARTER RATION

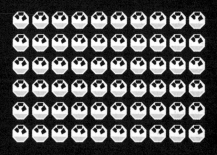

SIXTY RATIONS

CHARACTER
OUTFITS
IN *THE FORCE AWAKENS*

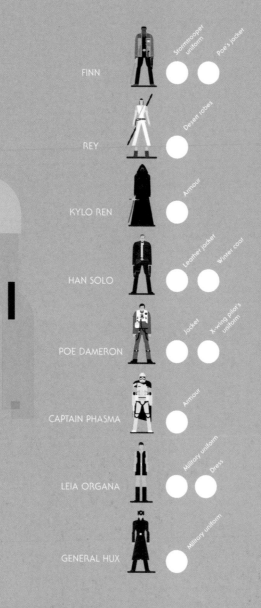

FINN — Stormtrooper uniform · Poe's jacket

REY — Desert robes

KYLO REN — Armour

HAN SOLO — Leather jacket · Winter coat

POE DAMERON — Jacket · X-wing pilot's uniform

CAPTAIN PHASMA — Armour

LEIA ORGANA — Military uniform · Dress

GENERAL HUX — Military uniform

SUPREME LEADER
SNOKE

KYLO REN

GENERAL HUX

CAPTAIN PHASMA

STORMTROOPERS

THE
HIERARCHY
OF THE FIRST ORDER

Despite his youth, General Hux rules the Starkiller Base and its garrison with an iron fist. But how does he compare to his infamous predecessor?

GRAND MOFF TARKIN

PALPATINE	**SUPERIOR**
EMPIRE	**ARMY**
GRAND MOFF	**GRADE**
DEATH STAR	**BASE**

DEATH STAR
MOBILE SPACE STATION

RESPONSIBLE FOR THE DESTRUCTION OF:

Alderaan

LOSES TRYING TO DESTROY:

Yavin 4

AFTER HIS DEFEAT:

Dead

GENERAL HUX

SUPERIOR	SNOKE
ARMY	FIRST ORDER
GRADE	GENERAL
BASE	STARKILLER BASE

RESPONSIBLE FOR THE DESTRUCTION OF:

The Hosnian
system

LOSES TRYING TO DESTROY:

D'Qar

AFTER HIS DEFEAT:

Alive

STARKILLER BASE
ICE PLANET

REY

GETS BY ALONE

The young Rey doesn't need anyone's help.
Here we look back at her journey.

Survives by her own wits
since childhood

Saves BB-8 from the grasp
of a Teedo

Escapes Unkar Plutt's thugs
when they try to steal BB-8

Pilots the Millennium Falcon

Finds Luke's lightsaber

Masters the Force

Escapes from prison

Fights Kylo Ren

Finds Luke Skywalker

EPISODE VIII

TRAILERS
& TEASERS

The release of the first trailer announcing the new *Star Wars* film caused a stir, but just how much hype was there?

THE FIRST TEASER TOTALLED

55,000,000

VIEWS IN

24 HOURS

THE SECOND TEASER TOTALLED

88,000,000

VIEWS IN

24 HOURS

THE FIRST TRAILER TOTALLED

128,000,000

VIEWS IN

24 HOURS

=

2 TIMES THE POPULATION OF THE UNITED KINGDOM

15 TIMES THE POPULATION OF NEW YORK

THE STORY OF
HAN SOLO
& LEIA

One fiery meeting gave birth to a magnificent love story. Here is the touching journey of the legendary couple.

A New Hope

Aboard the Death Star

The first time
Han and Leia meet

The Empire Strikes Back

Aboard the
Millennium Falcon

First kiss

Carbon-freezing chamber
on Cloud City

'I love you ...' 'I know'
Han Solo is trapped
in carbonite

Return of the Jedi

Inside Jabba's palace

The waking kiss

On Endor

'He's my brother' ... Leia
affirms that she only has
feelings for Han

The birth of Ben Solo

Kylo Ren

Separation

The Force Awakens

Takodana

Eravana

THE ASTROMECH FAMILY

FROM R-SERIES TO BB

R-SERIES

Versatile astromech droid line, particularly popular with pilots.

R-SERIES

R-SERIES

R-SERIES

R-SERIES

R-SERIES

R-SERIES

C-SERIES

Protocol droids programmed with many forms of communication.

C-SERIES

Before BB-8, there was a line of R-series astromechs – R2-D2 is the most famous example – as well as the C-Series. This page shows the progression of astromech droids to which BB-8 owes everything.

R-SERIES

BB-SERIES